Contents

Acknowledgment: Endpaper illustration by James Hodgson.

The Blue Book of
bedtime stories

Ladybird Books
Loughborough

Tonga the growling tortoise

by Bette L Vickers
illustrated by Petula Stone

Have you ever known a tortoise that growled? Yes, *growled*? Well, Tonga did! He was a tortoise that lived with the Dawson family, who were very kind to him.

The only trouble was, they had a puppy called Biff – and *he* was the reason that Tonga learnt to growl. Biff was always trying to play with Tonga, and sometimes he got a little bit too rough. Of course he didn't mean any harm – he was really a very nice puppy. He just wanted to play, and he was much bigger and stronger than Tonga, who couldn't move quickly because of his heavy shell.

Biff would go rushing towards Tonga, who would be out on the lawn quietly enjoying nibbling the grass, and he would roll him over and over like a ball. Sometimes he would even try to toss Tonga in the air!

Poor Tonga didn't know *what* to do. Rolling over and over made him feel sick. Being tossed in the air was terrible. It made him feel so dizzy that when he came down to earth his poor head just went round and round.

It was really very difficult for Tonga, because tortoises don't usually make any sounds and so he didn't know how to stop Biff being so rough. He quite enjoyed playing on the lawn – but not when it made him feel ill!

Tonga thought and thought about it. There must be something he could do.

He listened to the noises Biff made. He barked when he was pleased, but when he got cross he made a growling sound.

Oh if only Tonga could growl too and show Biff he didn't want to be rolled and tossed around! There was nothing else for it, Tonga decided. He would just have to learn to growl.

He knew this wasn't going to be easy. In fact it was going to be very difficult, for he would first have to find a voice to growl with. But he made up his mind – he would do it. And when Tonga made up his mind to do anything, no matter how hard it was or how long it took, he did it.

When no one was around Tonga would try very hard, and gradually he managed rather a good growl. It came from right under his shell, and when it was ready Tonga's head would pop out – his eyes would roll – his head shake – his mouth open and *grrrrrrrrrrrr*. A really *super* growl would come out.

At last, after much practising, Tonga decided the growl was good enough to stop Biff being rough.

The next time Biff rushed towards Tonga and was just going to start pushing with his nose – *grrrrrrrrrrrr* – Tonga growled.

Biff was so startled – he just couldn't believe it. He tried again and again and – *grrrrrrrrrrr* – Tonga growled. Even better than before!

Poor Biff. He stood very still, then he crept towards Tonga and licked him gently round his shell. Tonga liked this. He popped his head out and growled very softly. Biff began to understand that although Tonga wanted to be friends and play, he mustn't be tossed in the air or rolled over. And after this they understood each other very well and spent many happy hours playing together.

If you happen to be a puppy and passing the Dawsons' garden, do pop in and say hello to Tonga – he loves company. Especially now that he can talk to you!

The flower princess

by Charlie Chester
illustrated by Brian Price Thomas

There was once a beautiful Queen who lived in Primrose Valley. She was known as the Queen of the Flowers, and naturally her lovely young baby daughter was called the Flower Princess.

As she was nearly a year old it was soon to be the birthday of the Flower Princess, and her first birthday was to be a special one.

All the little elves and gnomes and dwarfs from the forest wanted to buy her some lovely presents, but the Flower Queen said: "NO . . . No one shall *buy* any presents for the young baby Princess. But," she said, "she will be pleased to receive any present that you MAKE with your own hands."

This proclamation set the whole woodland buzzing with excitement, and they all started to decide what they would make the little Princess for a gift. Each of them wanted to give the best present . . . and this is just what the Queen wanted, for they had been rather lazy and disgruntled lately. This will keep them occupied, she thought, and she was right!

They took a long time deciding what they would make, and finally some of them said: "We'll make a beautiful big cake for her with sugar and almonds and icing. It will be the biggest, loveliest cake of all."

Others said: "Ah, we'll be different. She won't be able to eat a cake, she'll be far too young. Let's make her a beautiful big doll's house, she will love that." They started at once cutting up the wood and sawing and planing and hammering away merrily.

Then a few of them got together and said: "We'll make her a beautiful party dress. It will be the finest dress a Princess has ever worn, with the finest silks and satins. She will look more beautiful than ever." They started to cut and stitch and sew.

There was a little group that said: "Ah, now she is a Princess and a Princess must wear a crown, so we will make her a crown of gold and silver and we'll make it glitter with diamonds." Each little group kept its secret about what it was going to make for a present.

There was one little dwarf called Noni . . . actually he was called that because he had no name at all . . . so they called him Noni. He was a gardener, and he was very upset because all he could do was to grow flowers. He couldn't make anything at all with his hands. It was true that he looked after the flowers, but everyone knows that you can't MAKE real flowers . . . not with your hands . . . you can only help them to grow.

One day, he was sitting looking most unhappy when a little fairy hopped onto his knee. "Why do you look so worried and sad?" she asked, and the little dwarf told her.

"I can't make anything. I am a gardener, I can only help things to grow and I did want to do something."

"What would you like to make for the Princess?" asked the fairy.

"I would just like to make her happy," Noni said.

"What a beautiful answer! I shall see to it that you will."

Noni the dwarf looked at the fairy for a moment, and she smiled at him.

"You *are* going to make something with your own hands," she said. With a wave of her wand she tapped the ground, and there suddenly was a little violin and bow.

"You are going to make music with your own hands, Noni," said the little fairy. " This is a magic violin and when you play it, you will make the flowers grow. They will spring up from the ground as you play . . . just try it and see."

The little dwarf could hardly believe his eyes. He picked up the violin and drew the bow gently across the strings.

Then, as he played on, he noticed that the climbing roses were climbing even higher, and when he stopped the roses stopped.

Noni laughed and clapped his hands with joy. "Thank you, little fairy," he said. "Now I can go to the Palace and make my present to the Princess."

The great day came when they all took their presents to the little Princess. When they all arrived she happened to be crying (she was only one year old, after all!)

"Just wait till she sees our present," one of them said. "She'll stop crying then for sure," and they uncovered the giant birthday cake. The Queen thanked them and was very happy and proud of them . . . but the poor little Princess still cried.

"Let's see what she thinks of our present," said some others, and they brought out the great big doll's house. The Queen was delighted . . . but the little Princess hardly saw it through her tears.

"This might stop her crying," said another little group, and they showed the lovely party dress that they had made. The Queen was overjoyed . . . and thanked

them too . . . but the little baby Princess was still weeping.

Next, the others showed her the lovely crown that they had made . . . and the Queen said how beautiful it was . . . and still the Princess wept on and on.

Then up stepped little Noni the dwarf and someone said, "What have you brought?"

Noni said: "I have these little plant pots full of earth."

"You can't give a Princess pots of earth!" they cried. They were going to push him out . . . but Noni waved his little violin that the fairy had brought him.

Someone shouted: "Any present given here has to be made with your hands only."

Noni replied: "Yes, I know. I am going to make music with my hands . . . just see what happens. Keep your eyes on those little flower pots."

They all stared at the flower pots and Noni the dwarf began to play. Suddenly the earth in the pots began to move upwards . . . then a flower broke through . . . and as the little dwarf played the most lovely flowers they had ever seen began to bloom in front of their eyes.

The sound of the music stopped the little Princess crying, and she too looked at the flowers growing. Then the little embroidered flowers on the coverlet of her bed began to grow too . . . even the flowers on the wall paper . . . and when they looked out of the window, the garden was a mass of blossom!

The Queen just couldn't believe it. She told Noni that his was the most wonderful present of them all and just right for a Flower Princess. "What is your name, little man?" she asked.

"They call me Noni, because I haven't got a name," he replied.

"Nonsense," said the Queen. "You not only have a name, you have a job too. From now on you shall be the Royal Gardener . . . what's more, we shall all affectionately call you GREEN FINGERS."

And to this day all the people who are clever at growing things in the garden are called just that . . . all in honour of a little dwarf who wanted to make a Princess happy . . . the little dwarf called GREEN FINGERS.

Ben
rescues a hedgepig

by Sarah Cotton
illustrated by Lynne Byrnes

Ben carefully put five empty milk bottles into the basket. Then he zipped up his anorak, put on his wellingtons, and went off down the drive to fetch the milk. It had been raining during the night, so there were big puddles for him to splash through.

When he got to the first cattle grid he held on tightly to the basket with one hand and held onto the wooden rails with the other. (A cattle grid is a deep hole in the road with iron bars across it so that people and cars can cross, but cows can't.) As Ben walked carefully across, he looked down into the hole below and saw a round browny coloured prickly ball, half hidden by grass and mud. It looked very odd. Ben had never noticed anything like this in the cattle grid before.

He hurried on down the muddy drive to the lane where the milk was left in a box each day. There were a few cows in the field and an old horse, but he was right up at the other end and was probably too busy eating to notice Ben.

Ben opened the lid of the box and took out five bottles of fresh milk. He took the empty bottles out of the basket and put them into the box for the milkman to collect in the morning. Then he put the full bottles of milk into the basket and set off back up the drive.

He splashed through all the largest puddles, then found a round stone which he managed to kick almost as far as the cattle grid. Just as he started to cross the grid, he remembered to look again at the funny prickly ball he had seen earlier. But it wasn't there!

He looked and looked and then went off to look for a long stick to poke between the bars. It *was* there: he could even see its little black eyes. He ran up the last part of the drive to find his mother and father, but then remembered the milk, so he had to run back to pick up the basket.

He saw his father first. He was busy sawing an old tree that had fallen down.

"Do you want to help me to stack the wood, Ben?" called his father.

"I will later, but first do please come and look," said Ben. "I've found something in the cattle grid. I think it must have fallen in and can't get out."

"Oh? What does it look like?" asked his father.

"Come and look. It's got lots of prickles and black shining eyes," said Ben, leading the way.

"It sounds like a hedgehog," said his father. "If it is I will need some thick gloves, otherwise his prickles will make it very difficult for me to pick him up."

They looked down into the cattle grid. There in the corner was the prickly brown ball.

"It's a hedgehog all right," Ben's father told him. "I've heard some people call them hedgepigs. Now, we'll need a few things. A box with some straw, and a bowl of bread and milk. Go and ask your mother for that, and I will look for my thick gardening gloves."

Ben ran off to find his mother to tell her all about his exciting discovery. He thought hedgepig was more fun than hedgehog, so that's what he called it. His mother found an old plastic dish, and gave him two slices of bread to break up into small pieces and soak it in milk until it was quite soggy. Then Ben went off to the orchard and took some straw from the bales that were kept in a dry shed there for the hens. He found an old box and put the straw into it.

"Where do you think would be the best place to put him?" Ben asked his father.

"It's not too cold; I think the garage would be the best place. We're not going out so he won't be disturbed. Leave the box there and we will go and rescue the poor thing. He must be feeling very wet and miserable if he's been there all night."

After putting on the thick gloves, Ben's father reached down through the bars and caught the little hedgepig before it had time to curl itself up into a ball. Ben was able to see his hands and feet, his dark eyes and little black nose. They put him carefully in the box in the garage, and Ben brought him the bread and milk for him to eat.

He waited and waited, but the little hedgepig stayed rolled up in the box and didn't move.

"Why don't we go away for a little while and come back later on?" suggested Ben's father. "He can probably still hear us, and is very frightened."

So Ben helped to stack the big pile of logs which his father had cut up, and then it was time for lunch. Just before he went into the house, he tiptoed into the garage, to find that the little hedgepig had burrowed into the straw and was almost hidden. He still hadn't eaten any of the bread and milk. Ben felt very disappointed.

After lunch he forgot about the hedgepig, because it had begun to rain too hard to play outside. Instead he got out all his soldiers and his castle, and was soon busy winning battles.

The afternoon seemed to fly past and it seemed no time at all before he was called downstairs to have tea.

"Afterwards, may I go out and see if my hedgepig is better?" he asked.

"Of course you may," said his mother. "Try not to get too wet though – it's still pouring down."

"Well, it's a good thing I saw him in the grid! He might have got drowned if he had had to spend another night outside," said Ben.

He struggled into his raincoat, then made a quick dash through the pouring rain to the garage. Opening the door as quietly as he could, he switched on the torch his father had lent him and again tiptoed to where they had left the little hedgepig.

Ben couldn't believe his eyes! The little hedgepig was standing by the dish of bread and milk and had nearly finished it all up. He reminded Ben of baby kittens with their little pink tongues darting in and out. When

the hedgepig had finished up all the bread and milk and licked the dish quite clean, he walked around his box for a few minutes, found a nice place to go to sleep in and curled up into a ball once more. "Goodnight, little hedgepig," whispered Ben. "See you in the morning."

He crept out again, then dashed through the rain once more, back to the kitchen. "Mummy! Daddy! Look," he cried, showing them the empty dish. "The hedgepig's eaten it all up and I watched him eat. He's gone to sleep now, all curled up under the straw. Can I leave him some more food for the morning, please?"

"Yes, of course, but only if you hurry," said his mother. "It's nearly time for you to go to bed."

So Ben took out two more slices of bread from the bread bin, broke it up into small pieces and filled the dish with milk until it was quite soggy. Then he carried it through the rain into the garage and placed it beside the sleeping hedgepig.

Next morning the sun was shining so brightly that Ben jumped out of bed and got dressed as quickly as he could. Then he ran downstairs, through the kitchen and out into the yard to the garage. But when he reached the box it was empty. The hedgepig had gone. But so had all the bread and milk he had left for him.

"Well, at least I gave you breakfast even if I didn't see you eat it," said Ben a little sadly. "And at least I did have a hedgepig of my own for just a little while." He went indoors to tell his mother and father what had happened.

"I'm afraid you probably won't see him again, because he sleeps during the day and hunts at night," explained his mother. "Why not leave a little of the bread and milk by the garage door every evening, and see whether he comes back to eat it?"

"Oh! what a good idea," said, Ben, cheering up. "Do you think he will?"

And that is what Ben does every evening, and every night when he's in bed and fast asleep, the little brown hedgepig always remembers to go to the garage for his bread and milk!

The mouse
who couldn't eat
cheese

by Charlie Chester
illustrated by Susan Edwards

Of all the tales in Fairyland – and there have been a few,
They tell just one that always seems to please.
It's quite a simple story, which I'd like to tell to you,
Of the little mouse who *never* could eat cheese.

This little mouse lived in a house, not very far away.
He wasn't very happy, for they teased him night and day.
The other mice would all make fun and every chance
    they'd seize
To laugh at him, and all because he just could *not* eat
    cheese.

Because he was so timid (Whiskers was his name),
All the other mice would say, that he had brought them
    shame.
They'd badger him and fight with him, and bring him
    to his knees,
And all because this little mouse just *never* could eat
    cheese.

Underneath the floorboards they would scamper all the
    day.
The older mice would sit and watch the younger ones at
    play.
Then late at night, when all was dark, they'd all come
    out to roam,
Except poor little Whiskers – for they made *him* stay at
    home.

"It's no use bringing him," they cried. "He'll change his
   mind perhaps,
When we have had a feast from all the cheese inside the
   traps."
Then off went all the other mice, to see what they could
   find,
And left poor little Whiskers all alone to stay behind.

They crept into the pantry and nibbled at the rice.
They finished off a crusty loaf and thought that very nice.
And all this while poor Whiskers went hungry, if you
   please,
Just because he was a mouse who *never* could eat cheese.

"I wonder if they'll bring me back a tiny piece of bread?
I'd even like a lovely piece of bacon rind!" he said.
"I'd love a piece of sausage, or some nice fresh garden
   peas.
I *wish* they wouldn't laugh at me, because I can't eat
   cheese."

The time went by, the clock struck two, the pantry was
a mess.

The mice had made a royal feast, and oh, their
greediness!

"Young Whiskers missed a treat," they cried. "*He* won't
get very fat."

They were so *very* busy that – they never saw the cat.

Back in the hole sat Whiskers, just trembling at the
knees,

And as the time went passing by, he felt quite ill at ease.

The other mice did not come home and there, as
Whiskers sat,

He learned that his dislike for cheese had saved him –
from the cat!

That little mouse called Whiskers, though he was only
small,

I think you know that he can be a lesson to us all.

So if you find you're different, don't let it worry you.

It doesn't always pay to do what all the others do.

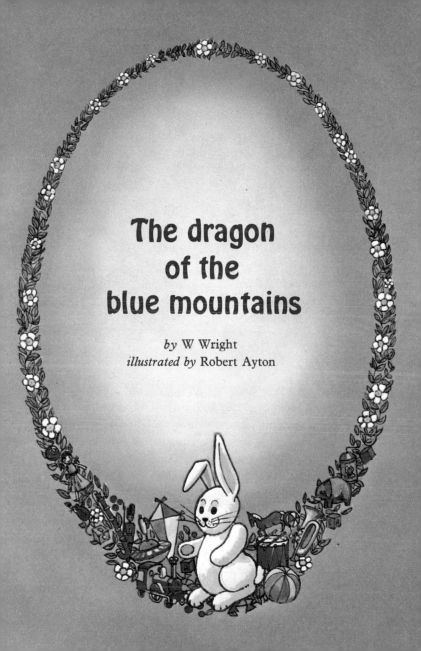

The dragon
of the
blue mountains

by W Wright
illustrated by Robert Ayton

On the side of a highway used by many merchants and travellers was an orchard, and in the orchard was a well of beautiful sweet cool water which was the only water for many a mile. Also in the orchard was a cottage where lived a lonely little man – at least he would have been lonely if it hadn't been for all the travellers who stopped at the well for a drink.

He had fitted a little bell to the well so that as soon as a traveller moved the handle to get some water from the well, the bell would ring. When he heard it, the little man would dash into his larder where he kept all sorts of lovely things to eat. There were pies, cakes, new-baked bread and

cheese. He would put them all into a basket and take them to the traveller who was visiting the well. The travellers were always very grateful.

"How much do I owe you?" they would ask, and the little man always replied: "Please tell me a story." A story was all he ever wanted in return.

One beautiful summer day along came a traveller who was very thirsty. As soon as he dropped the bucket into the well to get some water, there was a tinkle tinkle tinkle from the little bell. The little man heard it, and came out of his house carrying a big basket of bread, cheese, pies and cakes to offer the weary traveller.

The traveller was pleased. "How much do I owe you?" he asked.

"Not one penny!" answered the little man. "But would you please tell me a story?"

"I don't know any stories," said the traveller, "but a

funny thing happened to me a few days ago when I passed through the village at the foot of the blue mountains. It wasn't like most villages I pass through, happy and gay. It was silent, and everyone I saw looked afraid. So when I went to get some bread, I asked the baker why everyone seemed so frightened.

" 'It's because of the dragon,' he replied.

" 'I've heard of dragons.' I said, 'but surely there isn't such a thing.'

" 'There certainly is,' said the baker. 'He lives in a cave, halfway between here and the snow at the top of the mountain. That is why everyone is so afraid, because we are never sure what the dragon is going to do.'

" 'Does he hurt people ?' I asked.

"The baker said, 'No, he has never hurt anyone so far, but when the shepherd boys go up the mountainside after the sheep and the goats, he sometimes comes out and roars, a terrible big roar. Then he blows flames down and it terrifies the shepherd boys, the sheep and the goats and it frightens all of us in the village. Suppose he came down the mountainside ? Then what would happen ?'

" 'Is he there just now ?' I asked.

"The baker looked thoughtful. 'Well, that's the funny thing. We haven't seen him for a while. When the weather started getting warmer a few weeks ago there was a bit of an avalanche, and we haven't seen him since then. I hope we never see him again !' "

As the traveller told his tale, the little man was getting very interested indeed.

"I must go and see if I can see this creature," he said. "I have heard of dragons but I never believed that there was such a thing. Thank you for such a wonderful tale. How far away did you say the blue mountains were?" he asked.

"About fourteen days' walk along the highway towards the east. In about seven days or so you should reach a stream: follow it towards the mountain and you will come to the village."

The traveller left, and the little man started his own journey.

He walked for seven days until he came to the stream that the traveller had told him about. By this time he had run out of water, but there was plenty of water in the stream to quench his thirst. By about the thirteenth day he had no food left and he was so tired that he lay down by the side of the stream and went to sleep.

When he woke next day, he could smell bread being baked, and knew he must be close to the village he was looking for. Following the smell of the bread he soon found the baker's shop in the middle of the village.

"Where are you going?" asked the baker, handing him some bread.

"Well," said the little man, "I'm looking for the dragon. I suppose there *is* such a creature as the dragon?"

"There certainly is," said the baker. "Or there certainly was, but I haven't seen him for a while."

"Well," said the little man, "I want to go up and have a look at him, because I've never seen a dragon."

"You are a very brave man," said the baker.

"The traveller said that he had never hurt anyone and that all he did was roar and blow flames."

"That's true," said the baker. "He hasn't hurt anybody."

"How do you know he will then?" said the little man. "Perhaps he doesn't *want* to hurt anybody. Have you ever thought about that?"

"Well, no," said the baker, "but why does he roar every time the shepherd boys go up the mountainside?"

'I don't know," said the little man. "Why do dogs come out and bark? Why do the birds sing? There must *be* a reason, and I'm going to find out what it is. So I'll be on my way."

It took the little man all day to climb up the mountain-side until he reached the cave, then he found a sheltered spot nearby and went to sleep.

Next morning he woke early, and went to the entrance of the cave. He shouted, "Hullo, does the dragon live here?" There was a rumbling noise. "Hullo, hullo," he went on calling. "I hear that there is a dragon living here, a big horrible dragon who roars and frightens the shepherd boys. Where are you, dragon? Are you in there?"

Just then there was a really strange sort of noise. It sounded like "Boo hoo hoo", followed by "Splash."

"What on earth is going on in there?" asked the little man, and went further into the cave.

"It is me," said a mournful whimpering voice. "The dragon."

"The dragon? You don't sound a bit like a dragon! I thought dragons were fierce creatures."

"I *am* fierce," whimpered the dragon.

"You don't sound very fierce to me, you sound as though you are crying." said the little man. "Why are you crying? I never thought for one minute that a dragon could cry. What's wrong?"

"I can't roar any more and all my flames have gone out," said the dragon. "The other day I was at the entrance to my cave when there was a big rush of snow. When I turned round to see what was happening, I swallowed some of the snow and my flames went out. I got a sore throat and I haven't been able to roar since."

"It sounds like a dragon's cold to me. What do you want to roar and blow flames for anyway?" said the little man.

"Well, dragons are supposed to, and I haven't anything else to do."

"No, I suppose not," said the little man. "Have you ever tried making friends with anybody?"

"No one wants to make friends with me!" sobbed the dragon.

"I suppose no one wants to make friends with a dragon who roars and blows flames at them. I think we'll have to do something about it," the little man said thoughtfully.

"First of all, though," he went on, "I must make some sort of cough medicine for you," and off he went. After a while he came back with various herbs and some blackcurrants. He found a bowl and a large ladle in a corner of the cave and mixed all the things together with a little water.

Then he said to the dragon, "Now then, open your mouth and put your tongue out so that I can walk up it. I shall get a ladle full of cough mixture, carry it up your tongue and throw it down your throat, so don't go and close your mouth fast, or anything silly like that!"

"Oh no," said the dragon. "Of course not."

So the little man got a spoonful of mixture, walked very gently up the dragon's tongue and tipped the spoon. He gave the dragon several spoonfuls, then told him to go to sleep. The little man stayed all night with the dragon, looking after him, and every so often giving him a dose of cough mixture.

Next morning they both woke early. "Good morning," said the dragon.

"Good, your voice seems to be fine again," said the little man.

The dragon said, "Yes, but what about my flames? How can I get them back?"

"Well," said the little man, "what are you going to do with your flames if you get them back? Are you going to promise me that you won't frighten the shepherd boys or the sheep or the people in the village any more?"

"I promise, I promise," said the dragon. So the little man got to work with his herbs again and this time he made a potion like a spirit which he poured down the dragon's throat once more. Then he made a torch with straw tied on the end of a stick, lit it and stuck it down the throat of the dragon. There was a huge *WHOOF* and as the dragon breathed out, huge flames came from his mouth and the little man had to jump for his life. "I do wish you'd be careful, Mr Dragon," he said. "You nearly burnt me."

"I *am* sorry," said the dragon. "I didn't expect it. It was really wonderful but I won't do it again. Let's go outside for a breath of fresh air."

They hadn't been outside more than a few minutes before the dragon spotted a shepherd boy coming up the mountainside, and he began to roar and even began to blow flames.

This annoyed the little man for the dragon had broken his promise to him. He ran up the mountainside as fast as he could and soon found a big ball of snow. He started to roll it faster and faster down the mountainside, and then he shouted, "Dragon, dragon, look here." The dragon looked round and as he did so the snow went right inside his mouth. There was a hiss of steam and *PSST*, it put his flames out again. The dragon was annoyed and upset and began to cry.

"Now wait," said the little man. "Don't get upset and don't cry. You're making a flood all down the mountainside."

"Well, look what you've done. I'm just back to where I was before," said the dragon.

"You promised and you broke your promise," said the little man sternly.

"I'm sorry," said the dragon, "I really didn't mean to, but I don't know what to do. What *is* a dragon supposed to do with his flames and his roar?"

"I don't know about your roar but I do know what you can do with your flames – lots of things," said the little man. "First of all, though, how would you like to be friendly with the villagers instead of frightening them? Surely that would be better?"

"Oh, I would love to have friends," said the dragon, "but nobody will speak to me."

"I think they will if I have a word with them," said the little man. "Now we must get your flames back again, and after that I shall go down and see the villagers. You must promise not to roar or blow flames while I am down there, otherwise you will only frighten them all over again." The little man lit the dragon's flames again, then went all the way down the mountainside towards the village.

The first person he met in the village was the baker, who was very surprised to see him again. When he heard what had happened, the baker got all the villagers together and told them the story, but they weren't at all sure what to do.

"Surely," said the little man, "it's better to have the dragon as a friend than be frightened of him all the time. He can do quite a lot for you."

The younger men of the village agreed. It was about time they made a pact with the dragon, they thought. They decided to go and meet him.

So all the young men of the village started trekking up the mountainside with the little man. When they got halfway up, the dragon stuck his head out of the cave. He could see the little man, who waved to him and shouted, "Hey, come down, come down."

"Is it all right?" asked the dragon, so the little man turned to the young villagers and said, "Is it all right?" and they all shouted, "Yes, yes, come down."

The dragon was pleased, and he started down the mountainside. It didn't take him long for he took huge steps as he came thundering down. Soon he came to the young men of the village, and the little man said, "There he is, the dragon you've been so afraid of. He's not really a fierce dragon at all. All he wants is to be friends: will you be his friends?"

All the young men of the village said, "Yes, we'll be your friends if you'll be ours!" The dragon said, "Certainly I'll be your friend. I've always wanted friends and I've never had any at all before."

They all cheered, then said, "Let's go back down to the village."

"Jump on my back," said the dragon, "and I'll take you all there."

So everyone climbed onto the dragon's back and he took them down to the village.

When he got there, there was no one to be seen. The villagers were hiding behind walls, and houses, and the church.

"Come out," said the young men. "Come out and meet our friendly dragon." And one by one they came out, the old people and the young people and the children, to meet the dragon.

"There," said the little man, "that's the dragon who wants friends. Will you be his friend?"

The villagers in one big shout said, "Yes, we'll be his friends. We would love to be his friend." The dragon gave a huge roar, then said, "I'm sorry, I didn't mean to roar, it was just that I was so pleased."

"Don't worry," said the men of the village. "As long as you are happy, that's fine, we can all be happy then."

"Of course you can!" said the little man, and he looked round. "Where is the baker?"

"Here I am," said the baker. "I'm just going to bake some bread."

"Have you lit your fires yet?" asked the little man. "No, not yet," was the reply. "Well, there you are, Mr Dragon. There's a little job for you – stick your head through that big door there. You see that hole there? That's the fire to the bakery ovens; just blow some flames through there."

"Blow some flames? You said *not* to blow flames," said the dragon, puzzled.

The little man said, "You can blow flames just this once into that hole there."

So the dragon blew *Whoooosh*, and in next to no time the coke was hot, the bread and cakes were baking and everything was almost ready.

"Oh, I am happy," said the dragon. "Is there anything else I can do?"

The little man looked round. "Does anybody ever swim in that lake?" he asked, pointing.

"No," said the boys. "It is much too cold to swim in."

"There you are, Mr Dragon. If you want to be friends with the little boys, warm the water up." The dragon instantly blew his great big flame into the lake, *Whoosh, whoosh, whoosh.* "Is it warm enough yet?"

One little boy put his hand in the water. "Oh, it is just right! Thank you."

In a few minutes, all the boys were splashing about in the water. The dragon went on doing all sorts of things to help, and very soon everybody in the village liked him.

The little man was pleased too, because he decided to live in the village with all his new friends.

So they all lived happily ever after.